# NUMBER ONE SAM

**FOR ROTEM**

# DAILY ✳ BARK
## SAM THE BEST

TOP DOG WINS IT ALL!

★ ★ SPORTS ★ ★
## #1 SAM!

"Stay in School"

GO SAM!

FIRST FIRST FIRST FIRST

S
SAM

**1 SAM**

**SAM SAM SAM**

# GO SAM!

ISBN 978-0-545-91809-1

Copyright © 2014 by Greg Pizzoli. All rights reserved. Published by Scholastic Inc., 557 Broadway, New York, NY 10012, by arrangement with Hyperion Books for Children, an imprint of Disney Book Group. SCHOLASTIC and associated logos are trademarks and/or registered trademarks of Scholastic Inc.

12 11 10 9 8 7 6 5 4 3 2 1          15 16 17 18 19 20/0

Printed in the U.S.A.          08

First Scholastic printing, October 2015

● ● Printed in four spot colors. ● ●
Designed by Greg Pizzoli and Joann Hill
Hand lettering by Greg Pizzoli

# NUMBER ONE SAM

## GREG PIZZOLI

SCHOLASTIC INC.

Sam was number one.

He was number one in speed.

He was number one at turns.

And he was number one at finishing races in the number-one spot.

So on the day of the big race,
Sam wasn't worried one bit.

And he was number one at finishing races in the number-one spot.

So on the day of the big race,
Sam wasn't worried one bit.

He pulled up to the start,
wished "good luck" to his
best friend, Maggie,
revved his engine, and . . .

**They were off!**

Sam zoomed up to speed,
and nailed all the turns.

He and Maggie were neck-and-neck
as they headed for the finish line,
and then . . .

Sam lost.

Everyone
was cheering
for Maggie!

Everyone
except
Sam.

Sam couldn't lose!

He was the best at speed!
He was the best at turns!
He was the best at being
number one!

The night before the next race,
Sam didn't sleep one wink.

At the starting line, Sam was quiet.
The cars lined up.
The engines revved.

Sam didn't say anything to Maggie.

He was too nervous.

In fact, he was so distracted
he missed the starting flag!

Maggie and the other racers had a huge lead, but Sam quickly gained on them.

He was driving his best
and soon passed to the front.

Sam would be number one again!

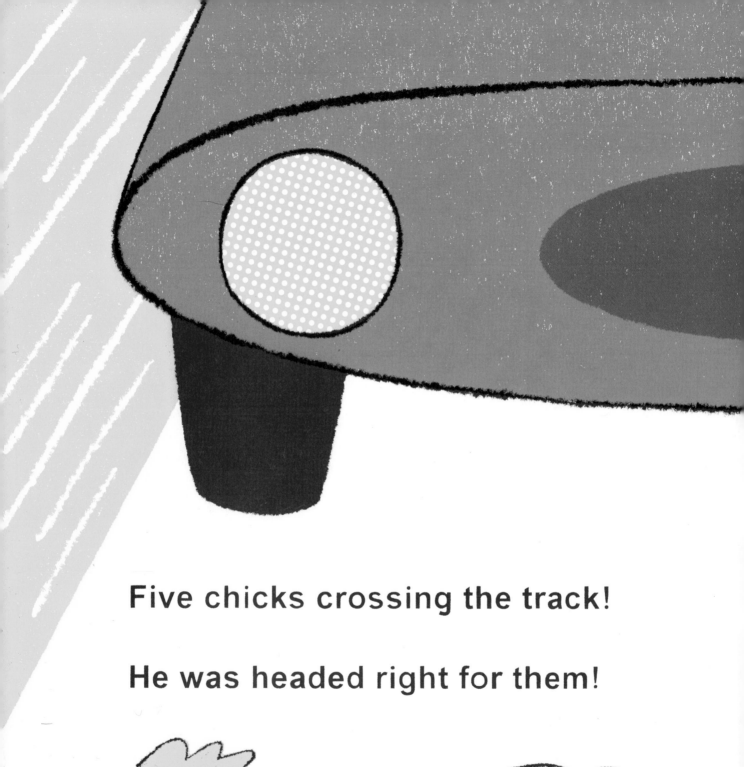

Five chicks crossing the track!

He was headed right for them!

But then he saw them.

Sam could steer around the chicks,
but would the other racers see them
in time?

Sam slammed on his brakes!

He scurried the chicks to safety as the other racers flew by.

Sam could steer around the chicks, but would the other racers see them in time?

Sam slammed on his brakes!

He scurried the chicks to safety as the other racers flew by.

Sam finished in last place,
the chicks thanking him the whole way.

Sam was disappointed.

As he approached the finish line, he heard people cheering for the other racers.

But as he got closer, he realized they were cheering for *him*!

And even though he lost another race . . .

# His friends still thought he was number one.